בס״ד
לד׳ הארץ ומלואה

This book belongs to:

Hachai

Please read it to me!

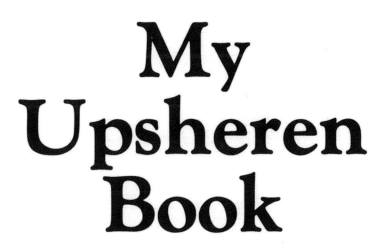

My Upsheren Book

by Yaffa Leba Gottlieb
illustrated by Binah Tirzah Bindell

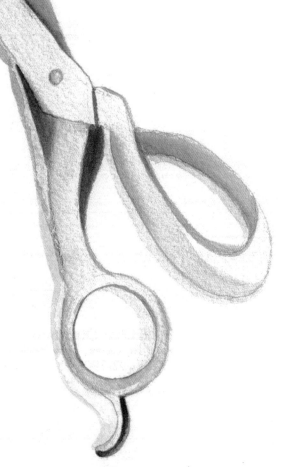

First Edition - March 1991 / Nissan 5751
Sixth Impression - Cheshvan 5781 / November 2020

ISBN-13: 978-0-922613-37-3
ISBN-10: 0-922613-37-0
LCCN: 94102075

HACHAI PUBLISHING
Brooklyn, N.Y.
Tel: 718-633-0100 Fax: 718-633-0103
info@hachai.com www.hachai.com

Printed in China

Note to Parents

It is a Jewish custom to refrain from cutting a boy's hair until he has reached his third birthday.
That first haircut and celebration is called an "upsherin" by Ashkenazim and a "chalakah" by Sephardim.

At this point, a child is considered to have reached the age of Chinuch, Jewish education,
and will begin to wear a yarmulke and tzitzis every day. He is lovingly encouraged to learn Torah
and to perform mitzvos.

During the Upsherin celebration, family and friends each snip off a lock of hair,
beginning with the area in the front of the head, where Tefillin will someday be worn.
Each participant has a share in the mitzvah of leaving the payos, side locks, untouched.

Numerous customs are connected with this very meaningful milestone,
and we have listed some of them here.

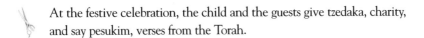

At the festive celebration, the child and the guests give tzedaka, charity,
and say pesukim, verses from the Torah.

Some engrave certain Torah verses on a hard-boiled egg and on a honey cake
for the child to eat.

Some have the custom to weigh the child's hair and give an equivalent amount
of silver or gold to charity in his merit.

After the ceremony, the child is wrapped in a tallis and carried to yeshiva
to begin learning.

The teacher spreads some honey on the page, and after teaching the child the first
letter, Aleph, the child will taste the sweetness and associate it with learning Torah.

An adult, acting as a representative of an angel (the Malach Michoel), showers
the child with candies and tells him – truthfully – that they come from above.

Source: Sefer Nitiei Gavriel

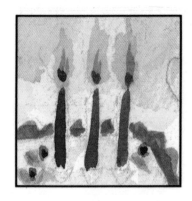

I'm going to be three.
I'm going to have my hair cut
for the very first time.

Here are the scissors.

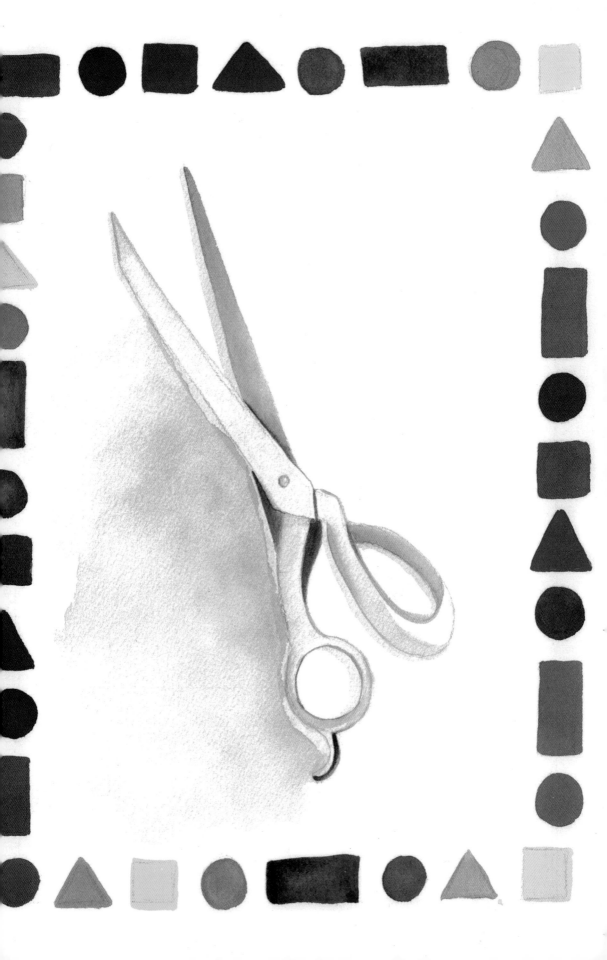

Here is the cake.
A special cake for me,
because I'm three,
and this is my upsheren birthday.

This is my new yarmulka.
I'm going to wear it every day over
my new haircut.
My mommy took me to buy my very
own tzitzis because I'm a big boy.
I'm going to kiss them every morning
when I say Shema.

Everyone is coming now.

My Bubbie and my Zaidie,

and my Bubbie and Zaidie,

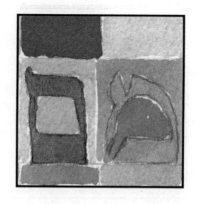

Snip, snip!
Now everyone takes a turn cutting
my hair. I won't have to wear
ponytails anymore.
Snip, snip! Snip, snip!
Be careful! Don't cut my payos!

Look at me! I'm really three!
"Mazel tov," everyone says.
I say, "Torah tzivah lanu Moshe,"
and everyone says it after me.
Then Mommy cuts my cake
and gives me the biggest piece of all!

Now it's time for Tatty to wrap me in his tallis and carry me off to yeshiva so I can meet my rebbe and learn the aleph-bais!

My first aleph-bais letters are
covered with honey. They are sticky
and sweet when I lick them.
"Torah is sweeter than honey,"
says my tatty.
Even the malachim are happy on my
special day. They are throwing candy
at me from shamayim!

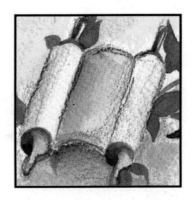

Who wants to learn aleph-bais
with me? I'm three!

Words That May Be New

Aleph-Bais – the Hebrew alphabet

Bubbie – Yiddish word for grandmother

Malachim – angels

Payos – literally, "corners." These are side locks which, according to Jewish law, cannot be cut off.

Shema – "Hear, O Israel" is a fundamental Jewish prayer affirming the Oneness of G-d.

Shamayim – the heavens

Tatty – Yiddish word for father

"Torah tzivah lanu Moshe morashah kehillas Yaakov" – A passage from Deuteronomy 33:4 that is commonly taught to children as soon as they can speak. It means: "The Torah which Moshe commanded us is the heritage of the Congregation of Jacob."

Upsheren – The ceremony of a boy's first haircut which, according to custom, takes place on or as close as possible to the child's third birthday.

Yarmulka – traditional head covering worn by Jewish men and boys

Yeshiva – school of Jewish learning

Zaidie – Yiddish word for grandfather